Published by Doubleday, a division of
Bantam Doubleday Dell Publishing Group, Inc.,
666 Fifth Avenue, New York, New York 10103

Doubleday and the portrayal of an anchor with a dolphin
are trademarks of Doubleday, a division of
Bantam Doubleday Dell Publishing Group, Inc.

Library of Congress Cataloging-in-Publication Data
Flack, Marjorie, 1897–1958.
Angus and the cat / told and pictured by Marjorie Flack.
p.   cm.
Summary: Angus the Scottie dog spends three days chasing the new
cat that has come to live at his house, but when the cat disappears,
Angus misses his new friend.
1. Dogs—Juvenile fiction.   [1. Dogs—Fiction. 2. Cats—
Fiction.]   I. Title.
PZ10.3.F594Am   1989
[E]—dc19   88-3626
CIP
AC

ISBN 0-385-07212-0
ISBN 0-385-07599-5 (lib. bdg.)

35   37   39   38   36

Angus
and the Cat

TOLD AND PICTURED BY
MARJORIE FLACK

DOUBLEDAY
NEW YORK   LONDON   TORONTO   SYDNEY   AUCKLAND

Each day as Angus grew older he grew longer but not much higher. Scottie dogs grow that way.

Now as Angus grew older and longer he learned MANY THINGS. He learned it is best to stay in one's own yard   and

FROGS can jump   but

NOT to jump after them   and

BALLOONS go

POP!

Angus also learned NOT to lie on the sofa and NOT to take SOMEBODY ELSE'S food and things like that.

But there was SOMETHING outdoors Angus was very curious about but had NEVER learned about, and that was

CATS.

The leash was TOO short.

Until one day WHAT should Angus find INDOORS lying on the SOFA but a strange little CAT!

Angus came closer—

The CAT sat up.

Angus

came

closer—

Up jumped the CAT onto the arm
of the sofa. Angus came closer and—

SISS-S-S-S-S-S!!!
That little CAT boxed
Angus's ears!

Woo-oo-oof—Woo-oo-oof!
said Angus.
Up jumped the CAT onto
the sofa back, up to the mantel
—and Angus was not
high enough
to reach
her!

But at lunch time down she came
to try and take Angus's food—

though not for long.

Up she jumped
onto the table,
and Angus was not
high enough
to reach
her!

At nap time there she was sitting in Angus's own special square of sunshine—

WASHING HER FACE,

though not for long.

Up she jumped onto
the window sill,
and Angus was not
high enough
to reach
her!

For THREE whole days Angus was very busy
chasing THAT CAT, but she always went up
out of reach until on the fourth day
he chased her UP-THE-STAIRS

into the BEDROOM and she was
completely GONE!

Angus looked under the bed—
no CAT was there.

Angus looked out of the window

into his yard,

into the next yard—no CAT could he see ANYWHERE.

Angus went DOWN-THE-STAIRS.
He looked on the sofa—no CAT was there.
He looked on the mantel—no CAT was there.
Angus looked on the table and

on the window sills—

no CAT was indoors
ANYWHERE.

So Angus was ALL-ALONE. There was no CAT to box his ears. There was no CAT to take his food. There was no CAT to sit in his sunshine. There was no CAT to chase away. So Angus was ALL-ALONE and he had NOTHING-TO-DO!

Angus missed the little CAT.

But — at lunch time he heard this noise:

PURRRRR—

and there she was again.

And Angus knew

and the CAT knew

that Angus knew

that —

Angus was GLAD the cat came back!